Who's that SLEEPING on my SOFABED?

by Ruby M. Grossblatt

illustrated by Sarah Kranz

Dedicated in memory of my beloved
sister-in-law, Phyllis Verner (z'l) who always
welcomed me to her home. R.G.

Who's that Sleeping on my Sofabed?

First Edition
Tishrei 5760 / September 1999
Second Impression
Elul 5764 / August 2004
Third Impression
Elul 5766 / September 2006
Forth Impression
Tevet 5771 / December 2010

The drawings in this book were painted with
Ecoline watercolors, on Schoeller art paper.
The text is set in Century Schoolbook 13.5
over 18 point.

Editor: D.L. Rosenfeld
Managing Editor: Yossi Leverton
Layout: Eli Designs

ISBN-13: 978-0-922613-90-8
ISBN-10: 0-922613-90-7
LCCN: 99-61438

HACHAI PUBLISHING
Brooklyn, New York
Tel: 718-633-0100 Fax: 718-633-0103
www.hachai.com - info@hachai.com

Manufactured in Hong Kong,
November 2010 by Paramount Printing

Yoni loved the blue sofa from the moment the delivery men carried it into the den and placed it under the big picture window. As soon as the men left, he pounced on the huge cushions.

"Yoni Block," said his mother, "take it easy or the stuffing will pop out." So Yoni took it easy. Stretching out lengthwise from head to toe, he looked up and watched the ceiling fan spinning round and round.

That night Yoni said "Shema," but he couldn't fall asleep.

His feet hung over the edge of his small bed. When he tried to stretch out his arms, one got stuck and the other fell over the side. There weren't any extra beds in the house where Yoni could sleep. Even guests couldn't sleep over.

Yoni grabbed his pillow and the fuzzy blanket his grandmother
had knitted for him when he was a baby. He headed for the den.
The door was wide open, and his mother was sitting there on the
new sofa. "Can't sleep," said Yoni.

His mother stood up and showed him a surprise hidden in the sofa. She took off the bottom cushions, Yoni helped her lift up the metal bar, and out popped a full-sized bed!

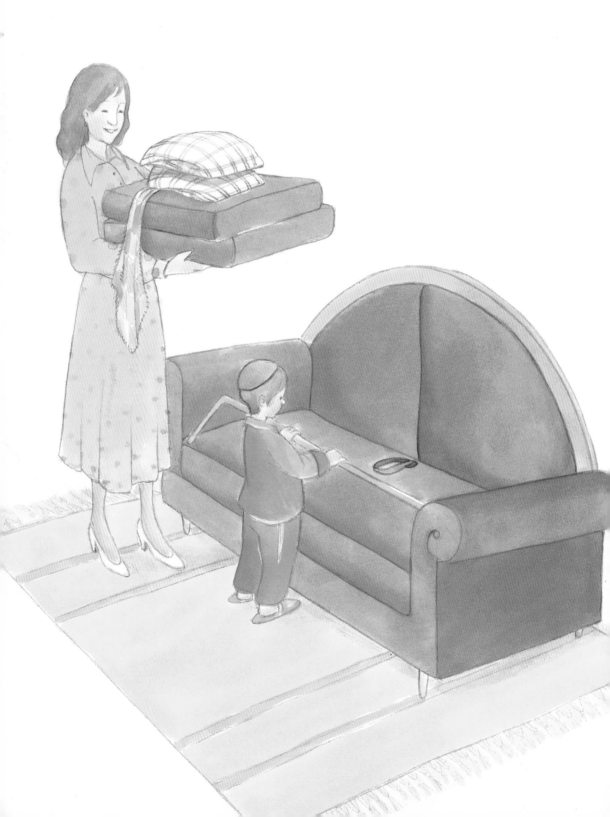

Yoni could hardly believe his eyes. The sofabed was much bigger than his own bed. He climbed in between the cool sheets and spread out his arms like branches of a tree. As the breeze from the ceiling fan ruffled his hair, Yoni fell fast asleep.

The next night, Yoni decided to sleep on the sofabed again.
He changed into pajamas and marched down to the den.
This time his father was there.

"Can I sleep on the sofabed?"
Yoni asked.

"Not tonight," said his father.

"Why not?" asked Yoni.

"It's a surprise," answered
Mr. Block.

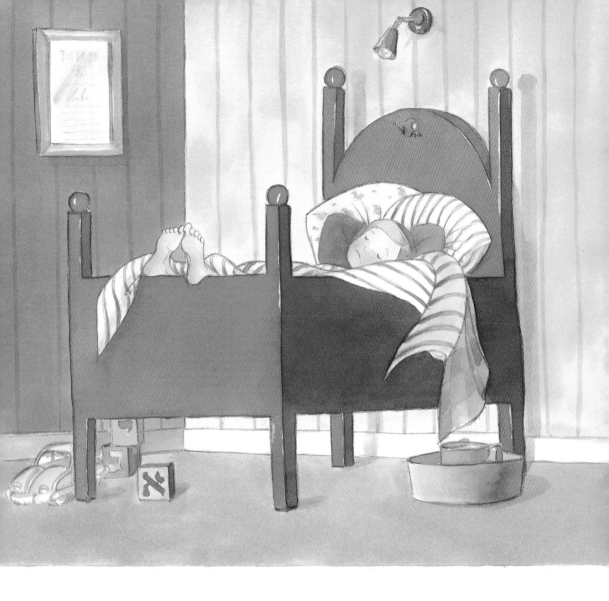

So Yoni climbed into his own little bed. His feet hung over the edge, and he couldn't stretch out his arms.

The next morning, Yoni said "Modeh Ani," washed his hands and ran downstairs. The door to the den was closed, so Yoni knew that someone was in there.

Yoni's father had already come back from shul. "Who's been sleeping on my sofabed?" asked Yoni.

"A Rabbi from Eretz Yisroel," said Mr. Block. "He's collecting tzedaka for his Yeshiva, and he needed a place to stay."

"Does that mean I can't sleep on the sofabed tonight?"

"That's right," said his father, handing Yoni a bowl of green and red apples. "But I am going to let you bring this to the Rabbi. Isn't it nice to have a guest?"

Yoni wasn't sure.

But since the door was now open, he walked into the den and put down the bowl of apples.

Next to the sofabed stood a tall man with a broad smile.
"Good morning," said the Rabbi. "What's your name?"
"I'm Yoni."
"Nice to meet you, Yoni. I have a student in my school
named Yoni. Would you like to see what he looks like?"
"Okay," said Yoni.

So, after he and the Rabbi folded the bed back into its hiding place, they sat down on the sofa and looked at pictures of the other Yoni and his friends in Eretz Yisroel.

The Rabbi said a bracha and bit into a green apple; Yoni said a bracha and ate a red one. Then they laughed at a picture of two boys who were making funny faces.

After a few days, the Rabbi left.

Yoni missed him, but he couldn't wait to sleep on the sofabed again.

That night, Yoni marched downstairs with his pillow and fuzzy
blanket. His parents were busy in the den.

"Can I sleep on the sofabed?" he asked hopefully.
"Not tonight," said Yoni's mother.
"Why not?" asked Yoni.
"It's a surprise," answered Mrs. Block, kissing him on the forehead.

So Yoni marched back upstairs, climbed into his bed, and stayed awake for a very long time.

The next morning, he ran downstairs. Again, the door to the den was closed, and Yoni could tell that someone was in there.

His mother was preparing breakfast in the kitchen.

"Who's been sleeping on my sofabed?" asked Yoni.

"A Sofer who writes mezuzos," answered Mrs. Block. "He'll be checking all the mezuzos in town. Isn't it great that he can stay with us?"

Yoni wasn't sure.

He davened and ate breakfast. Yoni's mother handed him a bowl of grapes to bring to their guest.

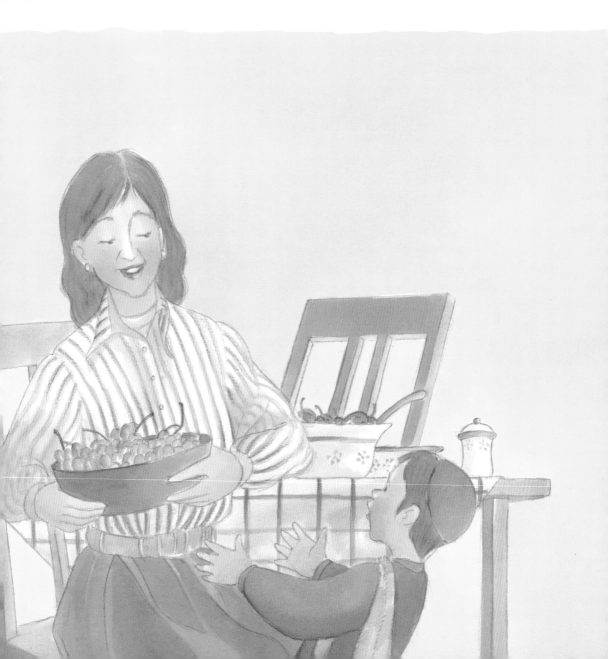

When Yoni tiptoed into the den, the Sofer was already working. The sofabed was folded up and away. Mezuzos were spread out on the desk in front of him.

"Good morning, Yoni. Would you like to write your name with a quill?"

"Okay," said Yoni.

The Sofer dipped the tip of a feather into shiny black ink.

He held Yoni's hand as they wrote all the letters in Yoni's name. On some of the letters, they drew a little crown. Yoni and the Sofer were so busy, they forgot to eat the grapes.

The Sofer stayed only one night. Yoni was sorry to see him go, and he missed the Rabbi, too. But maybe tonight he could sleep on the sofabed.

Right after supper, Yoni got into his pajamas. He even remembered to brush his teeth. Then, with his pillow and blanket, he marched downstairs.

"Please," Yoni called to his parents, "Can I sleep on the sofabed tonight?"

"Not tonight," said Mr. Block. He boosted his son up onto his shoulders and gave Yoni a ride upstairs.

The ride was fun, but it wasn't fun trying to fall asleep. His bed seemed to be getting smaller every day.

The next morning, Yoni ran straight to the den. Even before he got there, he could hear someone singing on the other side of the door.

"Who's that singing on my sofabed?" asked Yoni.

"A Chosson from Chicago," said Yoni's mother. "He's getting married tomorrow."

Yoni's eyes grew wide. "Can I go to the wedding?"

"Sorry, only your father and I are going." She handed Yoni a bowl of fruit.

"But it's a mitzva to make a Chosson happy," said Mrs. Block. "Isn't it nice that we have a sofabed so guests can sleep over?"

Yoni wasn't sure.

He put the bowl of fruit on his head and walked back to the den. The door was already open.

"Hey," said the Chosson as he folded the bed back into the sofa. "You'd be great dancing at my wedding!"

He grabbed Yoni's hand and hummed a lively tune as they danced round and round in front of the blue sofa. It was almost as good as dancing at a real wedding. Then the Chosson said a bracha and ate a plum. Yoni said a bracha and bit into a banana.

The next night, the house seemed so quiet. Yoni missed the Chosson. He missed the Sofer and the Rabbi, too. But maybe tonight he'd finally get to sleep on the sofabed.

Yoni changed into his pajamas, brushed his teeth, and marched downstairs with his pillow and fuzzy blanket. His parents were standing in the den, all dressed up for the wedding.

"Please, "begged Yoni.
"Can I please, please sleep
on the sofabed tonight?"

"Sure," answered Mrs.
Block.

"Of course," answered Mr.
Block.

Yoni was so excited as he
helped his father take off the
cushions and lift up the
metal handle.

He jumped between the cool sheets, said "Shema," and stretched out his arms. His mother closed the door halfway. Now *he* was the guest sleeping on the sofabed.

Suddenly, there was a knock at the front door. Yoni heard his father open it and say, "Hi, Ma!" That meant Yoni's grandmother had come to babysit. Yoni listened quietly.

"I brought a few things in my suitcase so I can sleep over,"
said Bubby Block. "Now you can stay at the wedding
as late as you like."

"Thanks, Ma," said Mr. Block. "I'll just carry Yoni up to his own
room, so you can sleep on the sofabed."

"Don't wake him," said Bubby Block. "I can sleep in Yoni's bed."

"I think it's too small for you," said Yoni's mother.

"I'll be fine," his grandmother answered. "Let Yoni sleep."

But Yoni wasn't really sleeping. He was lying on the comfortable sofabed with his arms spread out like branches of a tree, watching the ceiling fan spin round and round.

Yoni thought about his grandmother trying to sleep scrunched up in his little bed. He thought about his grandmother's feet hanging way over the edge of the bed and her arm getting stuck. Yoni gathered up his pillow and his blanket and ran to hug his grandmother.

"Hi, Bubby," he said.

"Aren't you sleeping yet?" she asked.

"No," said Yoni. "I want you to have the sofabed tonight."

"Are you sure?" asked Yoni's father.

"Are you sure?" asked Yoni's mother.

Yoni was very sure.

"Bubby is my guest," he said. "She should sleep on the sofabed."

"I think you're growing up," said Yoni's father. "Maybe it's time to get you a bigger bed."

Yoni smiled, kissed everyone goodnight, and marched straight up
to his room. He climbed into his own little bed, closed his eyes, and
imagined the surprise he'd prepare for his guest in the morning...
a giant bowl filled with red and green apples, bananas, plums,
and grapes!

GLOSSARY

Bracha - blessing
Bubby - grandmother
Chosson - bridegroom
Davened - prayed
Eretz Yisroel - Israel
Hachnosas Orchim - welcoming guests
Hashem - G-d
Mezuzos - parchments with the hand-written text of
    Shema affixed to the doorposts of a Jewish home.
Mitzva - one of the 613 commandments of the Torah;
    a good deed.
Modeh Ani - prayer of thanks said upon awakening
Shema - the "Hear O Israel" prayer declaring that
    Hashem is One.
Shul - synagogue
Sofer - scribe
Tzedaka - charity
Yeshiva - school of Torah learning